ASTERIX
AND THE BANQUET

TEXT BY GOSCINNY

DRAWINGS BY UDERZO

TRANSLATED BY ANTHEA BELL AND DEREK HOCKRIDGE

HODDER DARGAUD
LONDON SYDNEY AUCKLAND

ASTERIX IN OTHER COUNTRIES

Australia	Hodder Dargaud, Mill Road, Dunton Green, Sevenoaks, Kent TN13 2XX, England
Austria	Delta Verlag, Postfach 1215, 7 Stuttgart 1, G.F.R.
Belgium	Dargaud Bénélux, 3 rue Kindermans, 1050 Brussels
Brazil	Cedibra, rua Filomena Nunes 162, Rio de Janeiro
Canada	Dargaud Canada, 307 Benjamin-Hudon, St. Laurent, Montreal P.Q. H4N1J1
Denmark	Gutenberghus Bladene, Vognmagergade 11, 1148 Copenhagen K
Finland	Sanoma Osakeyhtio, Ludviginkatu 2–10, 00130 Helsinki 13
France	Regional Editions
	(Langue d'Oc) Société Toulousaine du Livre, Avenue de Larrieu, 31094 Toulouse
German Federal Republic	Delta Verlag, Postfach 1215, 7 Stuttgart 1, G.F.R.
Greece	Anglo-Hellenic Agency, Kriezotou 3, Syntagma, Athens 134, Greece
Holland	Dargaud Bénélux, 3 rue Kindermans, 1050 Brussels, Belgium
	(Distribution) Oberon, Ceylonpoort 5–25, Haarlem, Holland
Hong Kong	Hodder Dargaud, Mill Road, Dunton Green, Sevenoaks, Kent TN13 2XX, England
Iceland	Fjolvi HF, Njorvasund 15a, Reykjavik
Indonesia	Pt Sinar Kasih, Tromolpos 260, Jakarta
Israel	Dahlia Pelled Publishers, P.O. Box 33325, Tel Aviv
Italy	Arnoldo Mondadori Editore, 1 Via Belvedere, 37131 Verona
Latin America	Grijalbo-Dargaud S.A., Deu y Mata 98–102, Barcelona 29
New Zealand	Hodder Dargaud, Mill Road, Dunton Green, Sevenoaks, Kent TN13 2XX, England
Norway	A/S Hjemmet (Gutenburghus Group), Kristian den 4des Gate 13, Oslo 1
Portugal	Meriberica, rua D. Filipa de Vilherna 4–5°, Lisbon 1
Roman Empire	*(Latin)* Delta Verlag, Postfach 1215, 7 Stuttgart 1, G.F.R.
South Africa	*(English)* Hodder Dargaud, Mill Road, Dunton Green, Sevenoaks, Kent TN13 2XX, England
Spain	Grijalbo-Dargaud S.A., Deu y Mata 98–102, Barcelona 29
Sweden	Hemmets Journal Forlag (Gutenburghes Group), Fack, 200 22 Malmo
Switzerland	Interpress Dargaud, En Budron B, 1052 Le Mont/Lausanne
Turkey	Kervan Kitabcilik, Serefendi Sokagi 31, Cagaloglu-Istanbul
Wales	*(Welsh)* Gwasg Y Dref Wen, 28 Church Road, Yr Eglwys Newydd, Cardiff CF4 2EA
Yugoslavia	Nip Forum, Vojvode Misica 1–3, 2100 Novi Sad

British Library Cataloguing in Publication Data
Goscinny
Asterix and the Banquet.
I. Title   II. Uderzo
741.5'944   PN6747.G6

ISBN 0 340 23174 2 (cased edition)

First published in Great Britain 1979 (cased)
Third impression 1981

Printed in Belgium for Hodder Dargaud Ltd,
Mill Road, Dunton Green, Sevenoaks, Kent
by Henri Proost & Cie, Turnhout.

GAULISH VILLAGE

COMPENDIUM

LAUDANUM

AQUARIUM

TOTORUM

ARMORICA

BELGICA

LUTETIA

SPQR

GAUL
(ROMAN CONQUEST)
50 B.C.

CELTICA

AQUITANIA

PROVINCIA

The year is 50 BC. Gaul is entirely occupied by the Romans.
Well, not entirely… One small village of indomitable Gauls still
holds out against the invaders. And life is not easy for the
Roman legionaries who garrison the fortified camps of
Totorum, Aquarium, Laudanum and Compendium…

a few of the Gauls

Asterix, the hero of these adventures. A shrewd, cunning little warrior; all perilous missions are immediately entrusted to him. Asterix gets his superhuman strength from the magic potion brewed by the druid Getafix…

Obelix, Asterix's inseparable friend. A menhir delivery-man by trade; addicted to wild boar. Obelix is always ready to drop everything and go off on a new adventure with Asterix – so long as there's wild boar to eat, and plenty of fighting.

Getafix, the venerable village druid. Gathers mistletoe and brews magic potions. His speciality is the potion which gives the drinker superhuman strength. But Getafix also has other recipes up his sleeve…

Cacofonix, the bard. Opinion is divided as to his musical gifts. Cacofonix thinks he's a genius. Everyone else thinks he's unspeakable. But so long as he doesn't speak, let alone sing, everybody likes him…

Finally, Vitalstatistix, the chief of the tribe. Majestic, brave and hot-tempered, the old warrior is respected by his men and feared by his enemies. Vitalstatistix himself has only one fear; he is afraid the sky may fall on his head tomorrow. But as he always says, 'Tomorrow never comes.'

5

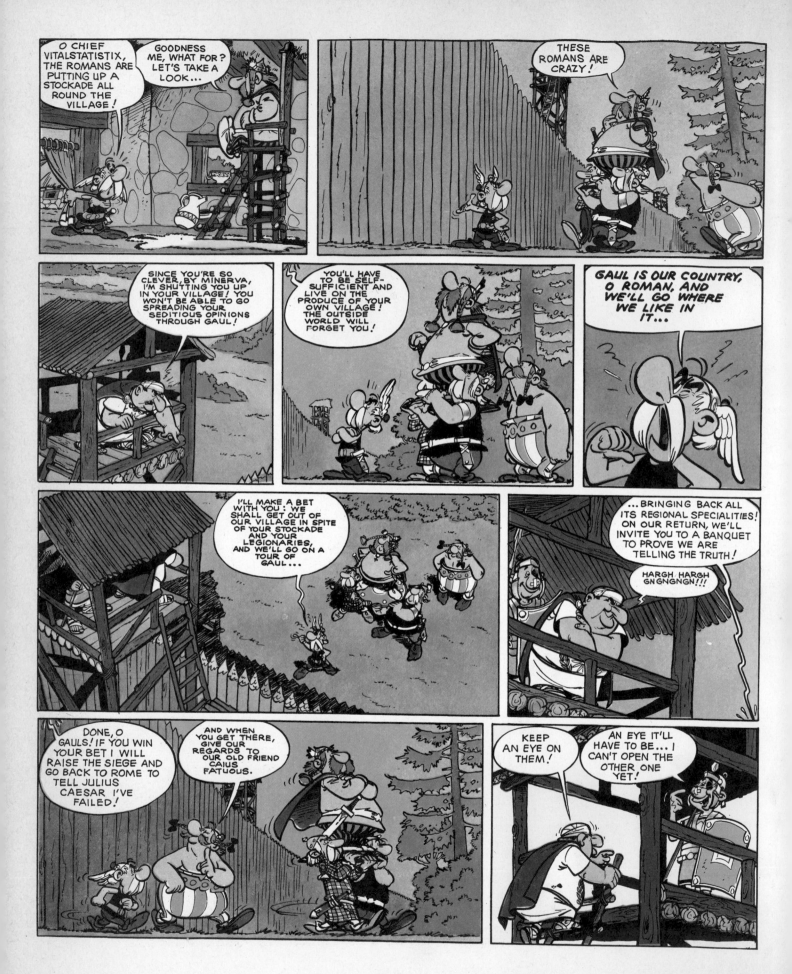

8

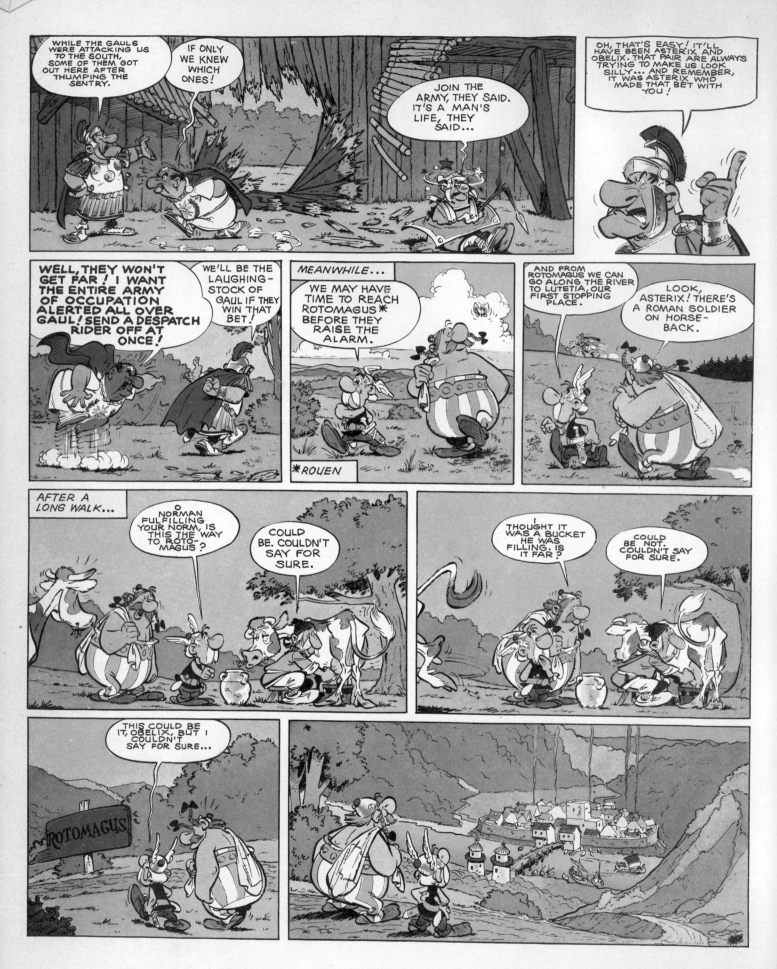

14

15

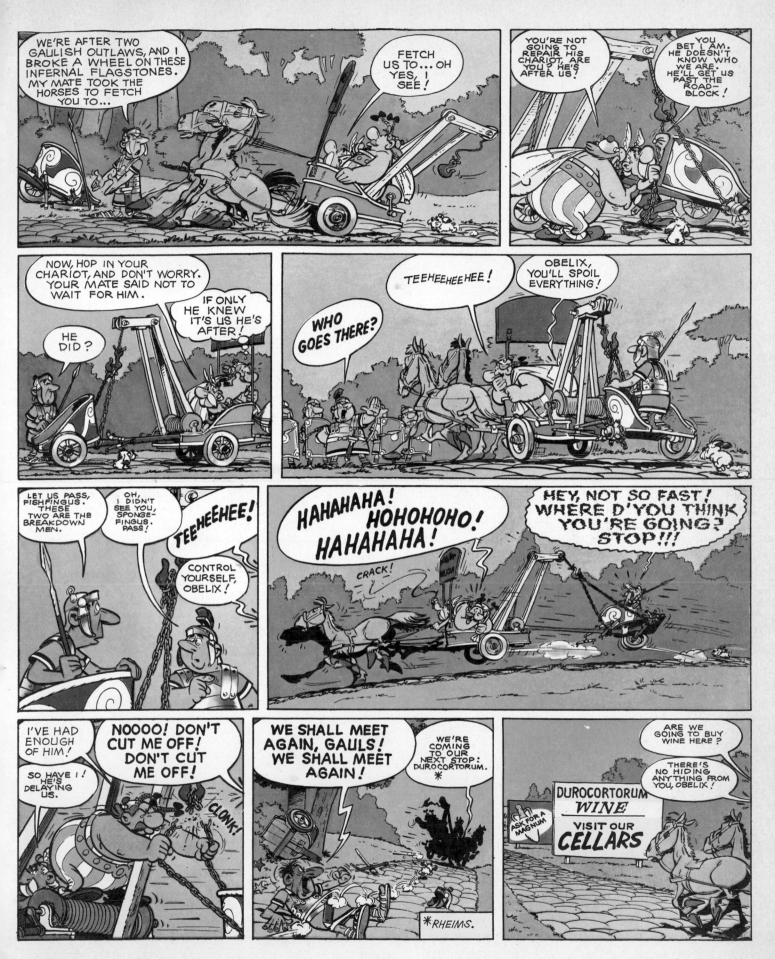

18

19

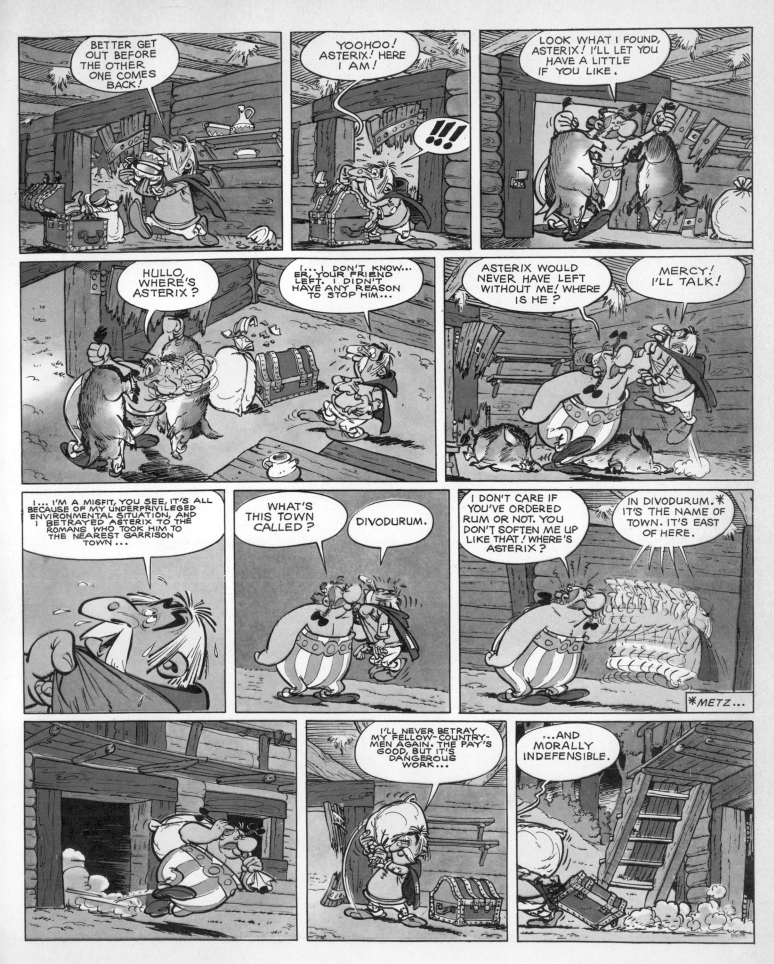

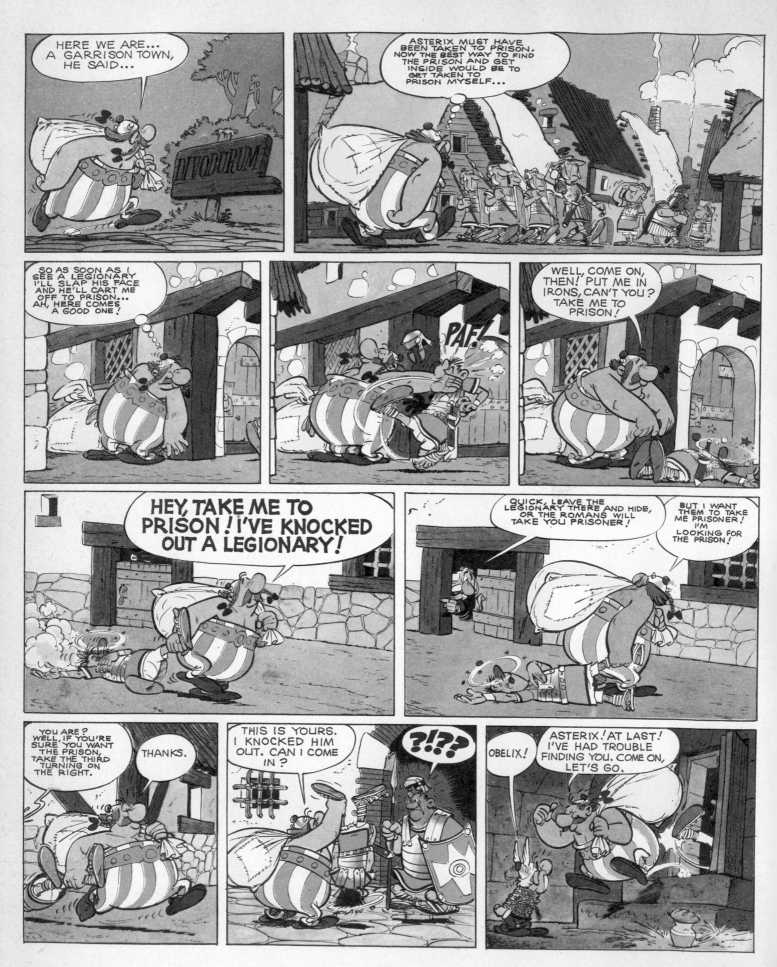

23

27

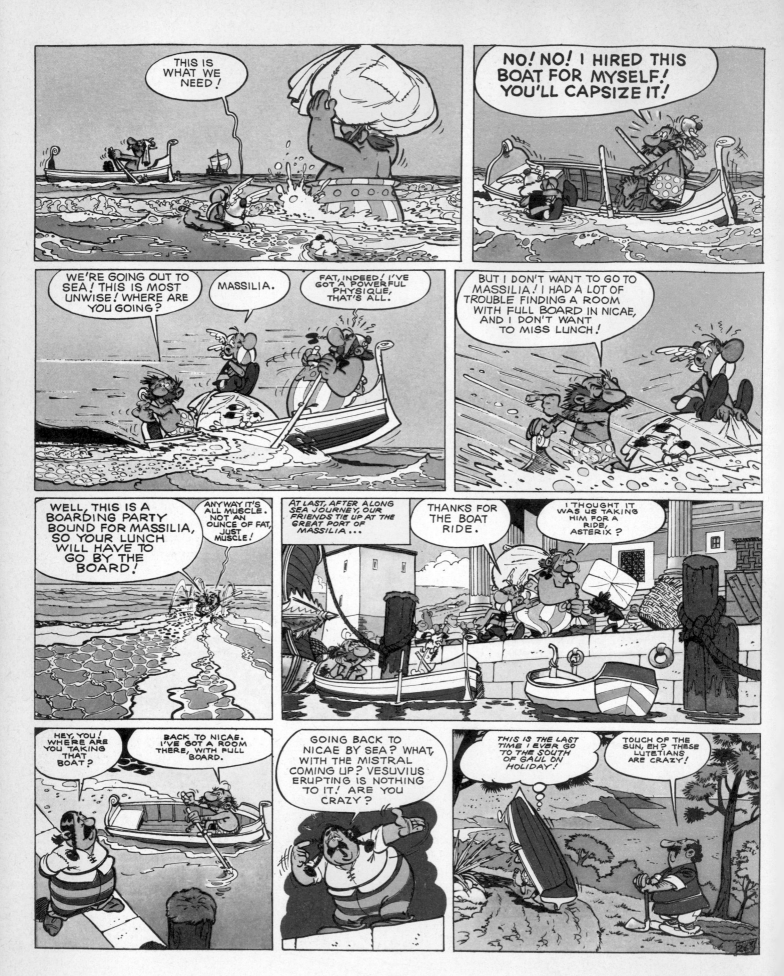

30

31

38

39

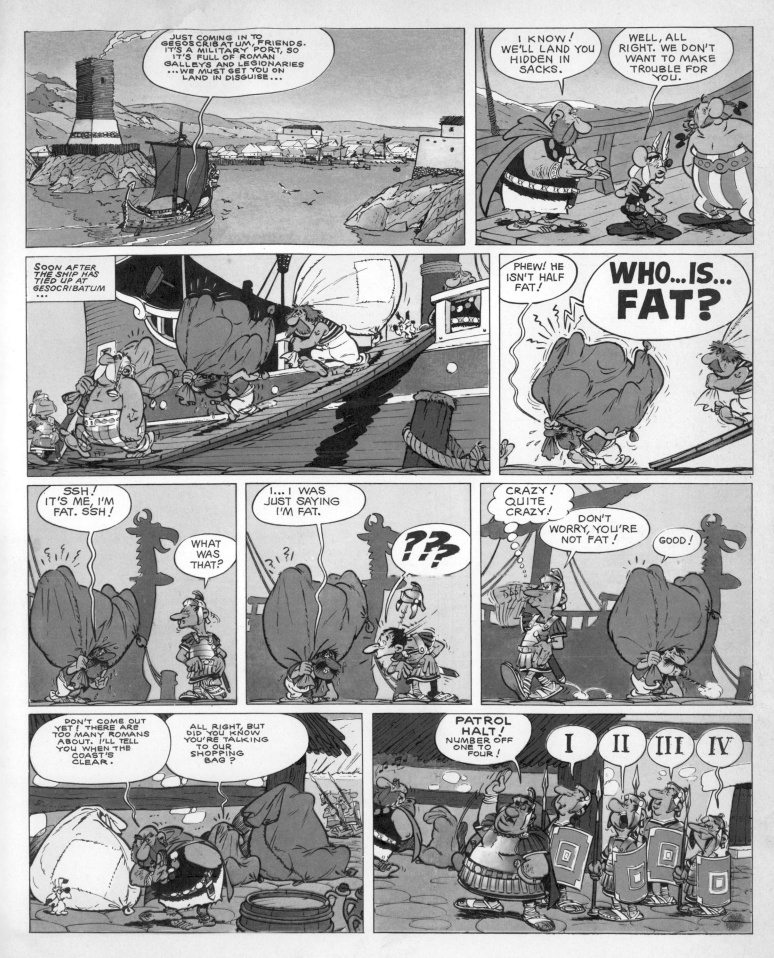

45

proost Turnhout (Belgium)

PRINTED IN BELGIUM